Deep Sea Dance

By

Kenn Nesbitt

Illustrations by

Rafael Domingos

For Mabel and Margo

Published by Purple Room Publishing
1314 South Grand Blvd., #2-321
Spokane WA 99202
Fax: (815) 642-8206
www.poetry4kids.com

Down on the ocean floor,
deep in the sea,

everybody's dancing.
Ready? ONE, TWO, THREE!

Barracuda boogies
with the octopus and eel.

Sea horse does a square dance
with the salmon and the seal.

Jiggle goes the jellyfish.

Shimmy goes the snake.

Everybody's dancing in the deep, deep dark.

But run away! Run away!

Here comes the shark!

Where did everybody go?
He heard the music play.

He must have missed the party.
They must have gone away.

Shark is all alone upon
this underwater shelf.

That's alright! Shark is happy dancing by himself.

He doesn't look so scary.

He wants to party too!

So barracuda joins him
for a bouncy boogaloo.

Jellyfish then joins in.

So do octopus and eel.

from the salmon to the snail.

But run away! Run away!

Here comes killer whale!